Copyrights Page

To request permission, contact the publisher at Publish@HurnPublications.com

Hardback: 978-1-7347634-9-2
Ebook: 978-1-7347634-7-8

Library of Congress Control Number: 2020946605

First Edition: October 2020

Edited by: Hurn Publications

Book Cover Designer: Diana Toledo

Calcado of Triumph Book Covers

Hurn Publications | Temple, TX

www.hurnpublications.com

Santa: An Interview

A Christmas Book for Families

Meaghan Hurn

HURN
PUBLICATIONS

This book is dedicated to my Grandma Jo, who taught me that love, acceptance, and patience are the most precious gifts in this world.

1945-2003

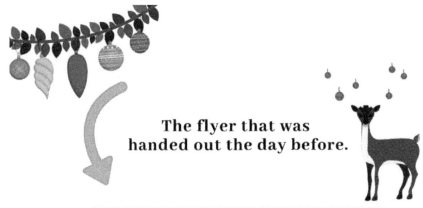

The flyer that was handed out the day before.

Santa Claus is Coming to Town

MEET THE REAL SANTA, LISTEN TO MY STORIES AND ASK BUT ONE QUESTION.

December 1st | Fairbanks Public Library |
6:00 pm to 8:00 pm

A Letter from The Writer

Welcome Reader(s)!!

I'm so excited that you're here!

You're about to read the pages of my notebook from the night that Santa came and visited my little town, Fairbanks, Alaska one cold December night.

You'll get to read along while finding fun doodles that I drew while I took notes. Since this is a notebook, there aren't any chapters, because this isn't your normal telling of a story.

I kept everything as I wrote it so that you could get the real experience of what it was like that night with Santa and all the town piled into our local library.

There's a surprise at the end and I'm keep that secret for now, you'll have to read through to see what happens with the proceeds of all the book sales!

Happy reading to you dear friend and thank you so much for reading our story.

May the Magic of Christmas Always Sparkle for You,

Raymond "Ray" James

THIS NOTEBOOK BELONGS
TO: _____ *Raymond "Ray" James* _____

Husband, Father & Journalist. In that order.
Please return to the Fairbanks Gazette Newspaper if
found.

Notes/Sketches/Doodles & Pictures
from the Night We Met the Real Santa Claus

NOTES:

It's a cold winter night, like most in our snowy village, and we've all come to our local library thanks to a small green flyer passed around the day before. It seems that the real Santa has decided to hold a town-get-together and has invited everyone to attend. This event is all anyone has been talking about so it's no wonder the place is already packed when we arrive 20 minutes before the official start time.

Along with me is my son, Ryan, who is 9 and my daughter Rebecca, who is 7. Both are practically bouncing off the walls and haven't stopped pelting my wife, Roseline, and I with questions. As a seasoned parent, I reply to most of their inquiries with, "We'll have to wait and see". I too have many questions, but the best journalists know when to ask and when to patiently wait for the answers to reveal themselves. Tonight, will be a test in patience for us all.

Our favorite librarian, Mrs. Yazzie, is greeting everyone at the door and helping direct traffic. We hang our coats, go to the restrooms, and get in line for hot chocolate and various treats lining the five tables in the back. Mrs. Yazzie is dressed up in her favorite Christmas sweater, a delightfully ugly red and white number, covered in Christmas lights that pop out and a T-Rex holding a sign that says, "I Rawr for Books!"; bells twinkling at her ears and a glow about her I usually only see when she's engulfed in a book. It seems the wonder and mystery of tonight has made everyone luminous.

We've located our spots on the floor, complete with pillows and blankets galore. Making it the most comfortable floor-camp-out I've ever been to, Snacks in hand and the last rush to the bathroom done, we all settle into our spots ready for Santa to show. Ryan and Rebecca are snuggled between my wife and me. And with my pen in hand, I hear the familiar deep rumble and jolly exclamation, "Ho! Ho! Ho!" followed by screams, cheers and happy shrieks of "SANTA!".

NOTES CONTINUED:

Watching my own children light up and become part of the magic brings a warmth and happiness to my heart that's hard to explain. Immediately, their faces light up and with big bright eyes they looked at my wife and I in awe, both loudly exclaiming, "It's Santa! He's really here!"

We all laughed, cheered, and clapped in a warm welcome for Santa and eventually settled enough to hear what he had to say.

Dressed in his famous red suit, complete with a full white beard, gold buckle and coal colored buttons, Santa made his way to the big comfy throne chair set in the middle of the room. He gave hugs, shook hands and gave a smile that reached his twinkling eyes to all that he passed. We were all enchanted. As everything calmed down, and people settled into their blankets, Santa took off his hat and sat down in his chair.

"Welcome to all of you" he boomed in his deep voice, "I am so happy you could be here with me tonight! This evening will be incredibly special. I thought it might be fun to take a short break from Operation Christmas and share a few of my stories. Each of you will get a chance to ask me ONE question, so be thinking on it. However, tonight is not just for the little ones. Parents, you should be thinking of a question as well. The magic of Christmas is not just reserved for the young, for you are all my family and I yours.

Now, let us begin."

There was an electricity in the air that's hard to describe as Santa started to tell his first story. To be sure though, every soul was listening, and he had our undivided attention. With a big gesture of his hands, Santa began.

SANTA:

Of my favorite stories to
tell, and the one I'm often
asked, is how I became
Santa Claus. I am very old
and was born a long time
ago indeed. In what is now
known as the Republic of
Turkey, in Myra, on a cold night just like this one.
December 6th to be exact! My parents were a lovely
couple that had wished upon the Northern Star for me,
every night. I entered this world as the first snowflakes
fell and found myself in a home full of warmth, magic,
and love. I was given the name Nicholas, and I felt
cherished every day.

Sadly, my parents passed away when I was only 9 years
old, but not before they instilled within me the love and
gratitude they had for life and in helping others. I
vowed to uphold their memories by bringing kindness
and magic to the world, as they so often did. They were
kind, thoughtful, generous, and loving. I was and will
always be their son and uphold our family values and
traditions.

I often helped the people of my village. Sharing meals
with those who had nothing to eat and was always the
first to lend a helping hand. I befriended animals
throughout our lands by nursing them back to health and

feeding them along my walks. I could usually be found chatting up the squirrels of the forests or checking in with the seagulls on the coast.

I went to school like everyone else, at the age of 11. I was accepted into the same school that my father attended. There are many specialty schools throughout the world that focus on magic and mine was in the Scottish Highlands. This is how a lot of the "Magic of Christmas" has come about. I learned all the basic things you would, like how to fly, levitate objects, and the ability to apparate. By far my favorite is the Undetectable Extension Charm I use on my Santa Bag so that it can hold all the presents for children around the world, without getting any bigger than its original size!

SANTA:

I went through my years of schooling, coming back to Myra on holidays, and as the year's past, I learned and flourished. It was my last year of school and during the last holiday break that I was given the title of Saint Nicholas. It should be said, my home in Turkey is surrounded by the sea. The Black Sea to the North is nearly impossible to swim in, because of the high amount of salt in the water, people who swim in the Black Sea actually float on the surface of the water. The Mediterranean Sea to the South is home to the Greek Tortoise, the Great Hammerhead Shark, and the intelligent Bottlenose Dolphins.

I was old enough at this point to be allowed to fly and had mostly mastered the art of it. It's much faster to fly from Scotland to Turkey than it is by horse or boat! I tend to stay high out of view, so as not to startle any non-magical people, but this unusual evening the winds were gusting from all directions and a storm had taken over. I would be safer at a lower altitude.

The ocean was choppy and huge waves could be seen, so most sailors would have made it to a safe cove by now to wait it out. You can imagine my surprise when I see lights off in the distance, smack in the middle of the ocean. I slowed down and drew myself closer, something in me knew they were in desperation.

SANTA:

As I got closer, I could hear the yelling of orders from the Captain and the groaning of the ship. This was a time before Emergency Lights, Alarms and Radios. The Ships were wooden and so, when damaged, elicit a strange groaning from the wood. High-Pitched snaps could be heard as part of the ship broke away. I dropped down onto the center of the ship, facing the bow and Captain. From there I could see sharp rocks jutting out of the side of the ship. They had run aground! I felt the rough seas pushing the ship further into the dangerous rocks beneath my feet and knew they were in trouble.

The sailors, shocked by my sudden appearance, backed away and looked to their Captain in disbelief. I hadn't thought what my immediate presence would look like to them and to be honest, we didn't have the time to worry about it. I looked to the Captain and he held my gaze. Questions burned in his eyes as well as the realization that we had more important matters at hand. A Brief second passed as we both understood the dire situation. If we didn't get them off these rocks and into deeper water, the ship would be battered to splinters and the sailors would be lost to the sea.

SANTA:

Without another thought, we jumped into action.
Together we re-tied and strengthened the ropes holding
the masts and worked with poles to pry the ship away
from the threatening rocks. It felt as if it took hours to
accomplish, everyone gave all the energy they had, and
we were chilled to the bone from the freezing waves.
Pushing against the rocks with our giant poles, it
seemed we weren't making any progress.

So, I looked to my left and to my right, made sure I
wouldn't be seen then twinkled my nose just enough to
send magic through my pole. It shot off with a strength
I hadn't meant to use and in seconds we were off the
rocks. A loud grinding sound could be heard as the ship
scraped itself off the rocks and into the raging ocean.
Cheering could be heard as we accomplished the
arduous task of rescuing the boat from imminent
danger.

As soon as the ship was freed and all sailors were at
their stations, I vanished. Staying within the area to
make sure they were able to set sail before finishing my
travels home.

SANTA:

Unbeknownst to me, the ship took refuge in the safety of a harbor. Not just any harbor though, they happened to be in Myra, my hometown.

The sailors were grateful and humbled to be on solid ground again. Imagine their surprise when they saw my face among the people in attendance. With whispered chattering and feet scuffling, they pointed me out to their Captain. I was unaware of this, so when he appeared before me, I was taken aback. The Captain looked deep into my eyes as if to clarify for himself that it truly was their savior from the stormy night before. I was a little shocked myself, and ended up staring back at him, my mouth a little agape. Happy to see them alive, confused that they were here; what were the odds that they would end up in my little village harbor?!

All that passed in a second, as the Captain asked me how I had heard them and been able to come to their rescue. I replied simply that a life devoted to others allows a person to be so clear-sighted as to be able to see others in danger and hear their calls for help.

They told the whole town what had transpired, and it wasn't long before I was given the title *Saint Nicholas*. I was humbled and honored.

SANTA:

It seems as though the accomplishments I've built so far were being recognized and I hoped others would follow in my footsteps of giving and serving others. Sailors reached out to me in times of danger and with my magical abilities I was able to hear their pleas for help. As the times went on and ships became safer and accompanied with more electronics, their need for my help waned. My love for helping others did not, however. It only grew.

I traveled further beyond my school and beyond my home country of Turkey. In each place I discovered new languages, new people, new customs, and beliefs. There were different religions and ways of dress, along with the most magical diversities in music, food, and art. In Dutch, my name is Sinterklaas, in France I'm Père Noël, and in England I'm Father Christmas. I look different to each person and speak many dialects. I became Santa Claus when I decided to help not only those in my town, or country or school. I became Santa Claus when I decided to help the whole wide world.

For my name means, "Hero of the People." and that is my life's calling.

Notes/Sketches/Doodles & Pictures
from the Night We Met the Real Santa Claus

NOTES:

Do you know that feeling you get when you listen to a really beautiful song? The kind of song that stops you in your tracks, makes you live in the moment and hear every note. Every trill of a flute, the melodic tones of the clarinets and booming of the bass drum gives you chills, your heart swells, your breath catches, and goosebumps immediately cover your body. That's the best way I can explain how it felt to hear Santa Claus himself utter the words, "For my name means 'Hero of the People' and that is my life's calling".

Tears welled up in my eyes as I allowed the feeling to overwhelm me and I looked to my wife to see her eyes glistening as well. Upon further inspection, it seems all of us were collectively sharing in this magical moment. It felt like the beginning of something big and there was no doubt, this was the one true Santa Claus. After a slight pause, that carried the weight of all our emotions, the veil lifted, and we immediately began clapping and wiping tears from our eyes. For here is the definition of a truly good person before us, and all he wanted was to give even more.

I looked down to Rebecca, while Ryan whispered with his mother and asked her what she thought. "It's Santa for sure, Dad! I just know it." she exclaimed. While the story had reached my heart and helped me remember the magic of this time of year, it had a similar and altogether different effect on our kids. It bolstered their belief in Santa even more and gave them the strength and courage to know in their hearts that Santa is real and not only that, but the magic is also real.

"I'm going to be thinking about my question. I want it to be a good one, Dad." she whispers to me. I respond with a similar whisper, "Take your time baby girl."

NOTES CONTINUED:

While we were speaking to each other, Santa had picked out the first four kids to ask him their one question. They were patiently waiting in a line, similar to when you wait to sit on his knee. Santa motioned for the first child to come up and ask their question. Rebecca gasps as she recognizes her friend, Sarah, headed up to see Santa. Sarah, a petite, curly haired girl of 7 made her way up to Santa and she wasn't the least bit scared of the saint that towered over her, even when sitting. An appreciative smiled formed on my face as she confidently marched up to the most famous person in all the world and asked him her question.

"Well, hello there young lady! How are you tonight?" Santa asks politely.

"Santa, I am really really happy to see you again!" Sarah declares.

"I'm always happy to see you too, little one. Do you have a question for me?" he asks, while inviting her over.

"Yes. I've been thinking about my question for the longest time and I know what I want to ask. How did you meet Mrs. Claus?" she chirps.

"That is a very good question!" Santa laughs. Sarah looks up to Santa with her big brown eyes, ready to hear the next story.

SANTA:

Well, when I met Mrs. Claus,
she had a broken arm and a
grin on her face!

During my 6th year at school,
I volunteered in what we
called the infirmary, better
known as the Nurse's Office, now. That was a busy year
for our school because we hosted The World Games on
our campus. So, throughout the tournament, I helped
our nurses bandage and fix many injuries, both serious
and minimal.

On the day of the final game, I was working in the
Nurse's Office, when she came in. Her team had just
won the tie-breaking game that made them The World
Games Champions! At some point during the game she
had collided with an opposing player and broke her arm.
That didn't seem to phase her much because she
apparently finished the game and celebrated with her
team on the podium before coming to get fixed up.

I remember her walking in, with the biggest smile on
her face and her blue eyes bright and happy. She
stopped me in my tracks that day, literally. One of the
nurses ran into me while I was just standing there. It
was quite funny now when we look back.

Finally, I shook my head to clear it, and led her to the
head nurse. We chatted and I kept her company while

she waited. I admired her fire and determination. And I think she appreciated that I enjoyed listening.

Mrs. Claus has always been an adventurous lady; athletic, intelligent, and quick witted. She was different than many people of the time and I couldn't help but fall in love with her. The rest is history as they say. We finished our schooling, wrote each other letters while we were in our separate schools, and upon graduation, we were married and began a lifelong adventure together. I'm proud every day that she is my wife. I am very lucky indeed.

NOTES:

Sarah, satisfied with her answer, hopped off Santa's knee with a quick "Merry Christmas" and a kiss on his cheek.

"Now, who is next?" Santa boomed. Looking to the little boy in line who seemed very shy, but stayed brave, nonetheless. Santa invited the little boy up and asked what he would like to know.

"Where do you live?" the little boy whispered. I would guess his age to be around 4 years old. He had a tightly curled hair, brown eyes, and a hopeful look. When asked his name, he shyly whispered, Jamal.

Santa seemed to sense his nervousness, because his tone changed to be softer and he answered directly to him as if they were the only two in the room at the moment. We had to listen very hard for the question and the answer.

SANTA:

I live at the North Pole, Jamal. At the tip top of the
world, where you can see the bright dancing flares of
the Northern Lights, hang out with reindeer, and build
snowman anytime of the year. We love it there. It's why
we have big coats, hats, and fun Christmas gloves. Mrs.
Claus and I usually sit by the fire almost every evening

There are roughly 100,000 elves living and working at
The North Pole. Everyone works together to create a
thriving town and a successful Christmas each year.
With this many elves, you can imagine how big our
workshop is and our whole village. That's why we use a
very powerful mirage charm over the town, so it's not
easy to find. The magic of Christmas is rooted in
believing in what you cannot see. Trusting in your heart
that it's there. That's the only way you'll be able to find
our Christmas Town.

NOTES:

The little boy smiled, and thanked Santa for his time.
Sliding off his knee only after being engulfed in a warm
hug.

Next up was, Yura. He babysits for us regularly. Smart
as a whip, 16, tall, athletic and had the honey-toned skin
of his ancestors native to the arctic lands, the Inuit.
Instead of sitting on Santa's knee, he shakes his hand
and nods his head as he offers, in his native language,
the question he has to ask

"What is your home like?"

In Yura's native tongue, Santa replies "Nakurmiik,
Yura." (na-koor-meek)

"What does that mean?" Rebecca whispered to her
brother with a sideways glance. Ryan shrugged his
shoulders while their mother answered for him, "Thank
you."

SANTA:

Ah yes, my home. I get asked this a lot actually and I always enjoy describing my home. Right now, even as we speak, my home smells of cookies. Mrs. Claus is always baking, especially this time of year. It's a two-story log house, with big glass windows, and is always decorated for Christmas.

Downstairs we have a big kitchen full of every baking gadget known to man, a dining room that magically stretches to exactly the amount of guests we have and our cozy living room full of welcoming chairs that seem to wrap around you and keep you snug. We have our bedroom upstairs; Mrs. Claus has a library that's her pride and joy and we share a small office as well.

Mrs. Claus and I like to redecorate the house every year. Sometimes we'll have a cozy warm atmosphere with lots of burgundy, gold, and wood accents. Other years we'll have a winter wonderland with snowflakes, light blues, and silver.

This year is one of my favorites! Every four years we deck out the house in a tropical theme, so we feel like we're having Christmas in the islands! The elves get into it too and we have a grand time! We eat more pineapples those years too.

NOTES:

Next up in the line was a 10-year-old little girl named Imara. Her hair in a braid that reached her lower back and more notably, her entire outfit consisted of unicorns. She had a great big smile that reached ear to ear, and her laugh automatically made you smile. Jumping up on Santa's knee she said

"Hi, Santa" and gave him a big hug.

"Ho. Ho. Ho! Hello, my dear. Thank you for a magnificent hug!" Santa exclaimed. "What's your question?"

Imara pondered for a moment, then said, "Where do all the elves live?"

SANTA:

Ah, very good. The elves love when I talk about them!
Each elf family has their own home, passed down by
generations or they build theirs with help from each
other. We work a lot with wood, so our homes have
beautiful wood carvings throughout. Every front door is
painted a different color and has its own unique design.
No front door is the same, like each snowflake that
falls.

The elves houses are always strung with Christmas
lights, candy canes and garland. They love decorating
and the bright glow from their festive homes lights up
our happy village. They really make the North Pole
come to life.

NOTES:

Having finished the first few questions, Santa was getting ready to select another three people to come up. Hands were raised, stretched, and waved to get his attention for their turn.

Santa scanned the room and pointed out three people, one of which being our very own. Ryan had been picked by Santa, and his first reaction was to stare back at us with wide eyes, as if to make sure it was for real.

I laughed, "Well, get up there, buddy! Go get in line to ask your question!" We wished him good luck as he slowly made his way up to talk with Santa and giggled to ourselves; excited to watch the exchange. Ryan took so long to walk up there, that he ended up being the last in line. Probably for the best, he still seems shocked that he got picked.

First up was Keiko. She seems to have taken advantage of the fact that we were in a library, because she walked up to Santa while holding several books. She gingerly set them next to Santa's chair and reached a small hand up for help.

"Hello, my dear!" Santa greeted her. "I see you enjoy reading! That's one of my favorite past times as well. What question can I answer for you?"

Keiko, cleared her throat, and clearly asked, "Are you really friends with *ALL* the reindeer?"

SANTA:

Yes ma'am! I am friends with all the reindeer. We spend lots of time together and we take care of each other. We go to the farm and eat plenty of fresh veggies, we go on walks together and get plenty of exercise. Just like everyone else, they have days where they're a little more tired and we stay in those days and read.

We like to read "Twas the Night Before Christmas" and "How the Grinch Stole Christmas" but our favorite book is "The Polar Express"

Each reindeer has their own unique personality, different things they are good at.

Dasher likes to go on walks,
Dancer loves to listen to music,
Prancer likes to dance,
Vixen is the fastest,
Comet is the funniest,
Cupid likes to snuggle,
Donner is the loudest,
Blitzen is the bravest, and
Rudolf is the most famous, but he doesn't know it.

NOTES:

"Thank you for your question, little one. Keep reading your books and tell me which is your very favorite next year!"

"Bye-bye, Santa" Keiko says as she picks up her books and holds onto them tightly.

Keiko's mom was right behind her and came up to Santa to ask her question.

"Hello Santa, we always like to leave a snack out for you on Christmas Eve. What's your favorite cookie?"

SANTA:

Always an excellent question!

I love all cookies; people tend to leave me chocolate chip the most. My favorite kind of cookie is one that someone baked for me with love. If you're thoughtful and kind enough to have left something out for me then I will truly love it and appreciate it.

NOTES:

Keiko's mom hugged Santa, said a quick thank you and was off back to her seat. Last up was our little guy, looking calmer now but still just as excited.

Ryan gets to Santa and asks politely if he can sit on his knee. I smile proudly that in all the excitement he remembered his manners.

"Of course, young man! How polite you are! Come on up here and let's hear your question." Santa exclaims.

Ryan hops up, wiggles slightly to make sure he's comfortable and looks to Santa "What are the reindeer's favorite snacks? Mine is oranges." Ryan asks.

SANTA:

The reindeer love carrots, celery, and oats.

Comet loves green onions, but they make his breath smell horrible. So, don't leave those out unless you leave some mouthwash too. Comet likes to be funny. He always manages to make us laugh.

Oranges are very good favorite snack choice. I love them too. We eat a lot of veggies and fruits at the North Pole. We grow what we can and buy the rest from farmers. Keep up the good work, Ryan, and keep eating healthy!

NOTES:

Ryan, thoroughly satisfied with his answer from Santa, gives him a great big hug, says "Thank you" and runs back into my arms, with a huge smile. I couldn't have been more proud of him. I know, as a little guy, that took a lot of courage to go up and do. Santa can be intimidating, just because he's so popular and well… magical!

Two more people were called up and the next question came from an inquisitive little girl, with dark braids, glasses, and big brown eyes. She politely asked Santa, "Are you really happy all of the time?"

SANTA:

Would you believe if I told you yes, I am always happy? I know that we all experience an array of emotions, and all of that is normal. We're allowed to feel upset, frustrated, or happy. For me though, I feel like happiness, true happiness, is not just an emotion we feel but an activity. In other words, happiness comes when you feel satisfied and fulfilled. A feeling of contentment, that life is just as it should be.

While the world may not be perfect, it does give me the ability to constantly strive towards peace. Happiness is like the Spirit of Christmas. It is a state of mind. If your mind is at peace, then you are happy. Because I strive to bring love, light, and joy to the world, I feel happiness all the days of my life, and you can too my dear. Excellent question!

NOTES:

The little girl, straightened her glasses, gave Santa a thoughtful nod and slid off his knee with a slight smile on her face. Clearly, she was thinking deeply on everything Santa had just said.

Next up was a red headed girl, with a small splattering of freckles across her face. She seemed to be about 12, comfortably dressed in her penguin pajama set. It was clear she was happy to be snuggled into the crowd and here this evening. She seemed to glide as she quickly made her way to Santa to ask her question.

"Santa, how can you be so old? Are you immortal?"

SANTA:

Ho! Ho! Ho! No, my dear, I am not immortal, but I am old! This is such a fun question, and one I enjoy talking about. To explain it better, I must tell you that there are many different kinds of magic. Your magic gets stronger with practice and experience. You'll find though that one of the strongest kinds of magic is the magic of love. Love is powerful and not easily broken.

The love of a parent is stronger than any other kind in this world. With my magical abilities, the collective love behind my good deeds that lead to me being named a Saint, combined with the Magic of Christmas, has created a very unique kind of magic that only seems to apply to myself, Mrs. Claus and the elves.

I learned in school that each kind of magic is different and has its own color associated with it. Love is red, generosity is green and so on. Since all mine are combined, they create a very unique kind of magic, it's a kind of magic that is the crackling and shimmering of light. This allows me to live for such a long time and ages me much, much slower.

NOTES:

With a wave of Santa's hand, a sparkling light shot across the room to the center and up to the ceiling. It burst into a shimmering snowflake and then vanished as if it were a firework. Immediately it started to snow, ever so lightly in the library. It wasn't cold, didn't melt and didn't collect on the floor. It was magical and only added to the awe and magic that filled the room.

The little red-headed girl exclaimed, "WOW!" as we all did and she slowly walked back to her father with her mouth agape, staring in wonder.

Santa pointed to the next three people and invited them up to ask their questions. They excitedly made their way over to his chair and waited their turns. One of the people chosen was a young boy of 15, who was in a wheelchair and wearing a brace. He seemed to have a permanent smile on his face, and I appreciated that. Since he was seated the closest to Santa, he ended up asking his question first. He announced that his name is Sam. Instead of sitting on Santa's lap, he parked his wheelchair next to him. Santa reached out and grasped his hand into his and shook it with gusto.

NOTES:

"Well, hello Sam! It's a pleasure to see you again. Might I just say, I like your wheels! You've decorated them very nicely."

Sam had wound battery powered Christmas lights around the inner workings of the wheelchair and had added a little bit of garland as well. He had fun with expressing himself and didn't seem to be bothered that he rolled around instead of walked around.

"Thanks Santa." Sam said. "I love decorating my wheelchair for every holiday. It's a lot of fun, and I love to be festive."

Santa nodded. "I couldn't agree more, young man. Now, let's hear this question of yours."

"Yes" Sam smiled. "I would like to know, where did all the elves come from?

SANTA:

Excellent question! The elves always love when they get more attention, since they are the hardest workers of Christmas.

The elves used to live in small clusters throughout the world. In places like Scandinavia, Germany, The Netherlands, and Iceland. When I setup shop at the North Pole and word got around that I was bringing the good children of the world toys, they enlisted to help. As the world's population grew, I ended up needing more and more help, so I was very lucky that they volunteered to be part of Christmas.

From all over the world they traveled to the North Pole to setup their homes and embark on this journey together. I could not have achieved so much without them, and the children of the world wouldn't have what they do if these extraordinary elves hadn't leant a hand. Mrs. Claus and I are truly grateful to them. Next time you meet one of the elves, make sure you give them a big hug and tell them Thank You. They really are a huge part of Christmas!

NOTES:

"I promise, if I ever get the chance to meet an elf that I'll give them a hug, Santa!" Sam declared as he rolled back to his spot near his mom.

Next up was Francisco, a boy of about 6 years old, with jet black hair spiked up to look just like his Dad's, who helped him up on Santa's lap, and waited patiently to the side for his son.

"Hi Santa" he almost whispered. You could tell he was nervous but with his Dad close by he was a little braver.

"How are you today, young sir?" Santa beamed.

"I'm good. A little nervous but Dad said that's OK." Sam replied.

"Your father is right. There is nothing wrong with being nervous. I'm glad you still raised your hand to come up and talk to me. Can I answer a question for you?" Santa inquired.

"Yes sir. I just wanted to ask, are the elves happy at the North Pole?"

SANTA:

That's a very considerate question of you to ask. I have to say, most people don't often ask how the elves are or if they are happy. It makes me very pleased to hear how thoughtful you are.

To answer your question, the elves are happiest at the North Pole. With our combined magic, the location is hard to find, which means they can roam about freely without worrying about being seen. They're very secretive and careful with their magic, so when away from the North Pole you won't see them unless they want you to.

Sometimes they'll go around the world to visit, take some time off and relax. Other times, they'll be checking in to make sure each child is being good. Each elf gets to choose what they want to do, build their own homes, take vacations, get married, have a family, read books, the list goes on really. They are very happy, and I know they appreciate you asking about them.

NOTES:

Francisco thanked Santa and sat down to wait for his Dad to ask Santa his question.

Francisco's Dad, Antonio, was up next. "Hello good sir!" Santa boomed. "You have a very kind-hearted son. I'm sure you're very proud of him."

"Yes, I am! He makes me proud every day." Antonio beamed.

"What can I answer for you?" Santa asked.

Antonio, winked at his son and said, "Do the elves only make toys?"

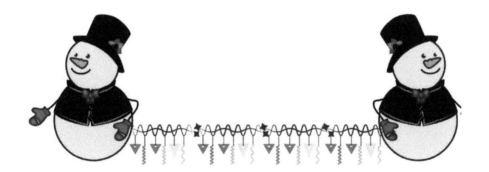

SANTA:

Ho. Ho. Ho. I see you and your son worked out your questions together. How charming!

With the North Pole having about 100,000 elves, it's safe to say that they all do not make toys. Here are just some examples of what our elves can do. Keep in mind though that they have all gone through school before entering the workforce and each elf gets to choose what it is that they would like to do.

It's estimated that the North Pole is where 67% of the world's candy canes are created. Chocolate; cookies; sugared almonds; there's no end to the treats our Chef Elves can design. There are Development Chefs for the experimental kitchen, specialist Pastry Chefs who work with chocolates to create intricate delights, and of course Caterers to keep everyone fed.

SANTA:

Another classic job for an elf is the Reindeer Keeper. It is a highly sought-after position, and as such, competition for this one is tough. Qualifications-wise, a degree in Zoology will help, as does experience as a Stable-hand, Zookeeper, or Veterinarian.

Another highly competitive career is the role of Santa's official Sleigh Mechanic. This is a very challenging task once you consider that the sleigh flies at nearly the speed of light, and it runs on magic.

To keep the sleigh in working order, we require experienced Mechanics, Engineers, and Aviation Technicians with a degree in Mechanical Engineering or similar experience.

SANTA:

The Christmas Sleigh doesn't just get used at Christmas, in fact, it's my favorite way to travel. Even in a sparsely populated area like the North Pole, there is still quite a lot of air traffic, so we have to be careful and check in so we're always safe and following the rules, like pilots do. That's why we have Air-Traffic Control Elves.

For this reason, our town incorporated a flight control tower, where elves ensure that air traffic stays safely separated. As this is a highly specialized job role, the elves use a specialist recruitment agency to get hold of the right elves here.

Farmer Elves are as important to us as anyone. They've designed Aero-Farming techniques so they can grow all the veggies and fruits needed to feed the residents of the North Pole. During Christmas, the Chef Elves produce tons of candy for the whole world while the Farmer Elves make sure they eat fresh veggies. A candy cane a few times a year is considered a treat. It's not what we eat every day. These farmers work together to grow foods in this cold climate by doing so indoors.

SANTA:

You see, our Christmas Town is much like any other town in the world. We have all different kinds of jobs, from elves that create our Daily Newspaper to those who paint and create amazing Christmas Art, and everything in between.

The elves choose who they want to be and have their own colleges and trade schools just like anywhere else in the world.

NOTES:

This continued for quite a while, children and adults would ask their questions of Santa and he would excitedly answer each one fully, taking the time to give each person his undivided attention.

He answered many of the questions we often hear,

"How do you visit every child in the world?" and

"How do you REALLY know if we've been bad or good?"

NOTES CONTINUED:

My wife and I decided not to ask questions, and instead we enjoyed the exchanges around us, happy in the honor of being present to witness it all. Our town may be small, but with the amount of questions asked I felt we would go well into the night, but upon looking at the clock, I could see it was only just now 9:00 pm. I had my suspicions that this was Santa's doing.

As the night was ending, the crowd had mainly asked their questions, and the remaining five kids were in line, patiently waiting their turn.

I could see the twinkle in the next child's eye, he just vibrated with excitement and you knew he couldn't wait to ask his question. Little Billy, known well in my daughter's class for being the class clown kept you on your toes in the best possible way.

He had succinct questions that caught you off guard and he always had a joke for you. It was a tossup on which one of these he'd be throwing out at Santa.

SANTA:

"Well, now, young man, what can I answer for you?" bellowed Santa as he helped Billy up to his lap so they could converse on the same level.

Billy, without missing a beat and with absolutely no shyness at all asked, 'Santa, what's your favorite joke?"

"Ho! Ho! Ho! I do love a good laugh. It keeps you young at heart! Now, let me think. What is my favorite joke? Naturally, it's Christmas related. Oh! Yes, I've got it!"

"What does Mrs. Claus say to Santa when there are clouds in the sky?" Santa paused to see if Billy knew. When Billy smiled and shrugged his shoulders Santa answered, "It looks like rain, deer." And they both giggled together.

"You want to know that's my favorite joke, Billy?" Santa asked. Billy nodded, "Yeah!"

SANTA:

"Because Mrs. Claus really does that and we both laugh together every time. It never gets old!"

"Now, tell me your favorite Christmas joke." Santa said to Billy, which I think he'd been hoping for, because his face lit up even more.

"What do snowmen eat for breakfast?!" Billy asked. Santa followed up with the same shrug and smile that Billy responded with earlier, so he answered, "Snowflakes!" and they both fell back into a fit of giggles.

NOTES:

Billy ran off, after he gave Santa a high-five, and his smile lit up the room. Each child's excitement before and after they spoke with Santa added more magic to the small space, we all filled here in the library and it only continued to grow.

Isabella was next, she had seemed sleepy while waiting in line, but she was now wide awake with the anticipation of talking with Santa. She was a little shorter, so she hopped up onto the arm of Santa's chair, so that they were face to face.

SANTA:

"Wonderful Isabella, what question may I answer for you?" Santa smiled at her.

Isabella smiled back, one of her front teeth missing and dimples in both cheeks, and asked "What do you do the rest of the year?"

"Well, right before Christmas, I take a short break to recharge and get ready for the huge trip I have to make and right after Christmas our whole town slows down and we all work on recharging ourselves after the craziness of the months leading up to Christmas.

Throughout the year I travel to help far away countries that don't have much and need our help. Mrs. Claus and I love to give back to the world, so we strive to help in any way we're able to. She makes blankets and clothes for kids in foster care and those up for adoption, waiting for their forever homes to find them. I often travel to Santa Schools around the world to help the amazing volunteers learn the art of being the Spirit of Christmas. It's a wonderful life for us and we enjoy giving to the world year-round."

NOTES:

Next was our little Rebecca, she was my mini me when it came to journalism and she often wanted to come to work with me so she can pester the weather anchors with her questions. I had a fairly good idea what her question might be about.

SANTA:

"Miss Rebecca! How are you little one! Come on up, let's hear your question." Santa boomed and Rebecca made her way up the massive chair.

Straightening her skirt and then finally her glasses, she looked at Santa and asked, "What do you do in bad weather when you're delivering presents?"

"Magic!" Santa answered. "Magic is how I deal with bad weather and I'm lucky to have such an option. The winds are particularly rough when we fly overseas and freezing cold too. A simple charm helps keep the wind, rain, snow and cold from pelting through our winter clothes and freezing us."

NOTES:

Yup, not surprised at all. Rebecca's face was quite entertaining. Part of her really had wanted a more scientific answer but she understood this was Santa and he was separate from logic and science. He was magic and love and this just was how it was when it came to how he accomplished such amazing feats.

Second to last, and already up on Santa's chair, is Justin. He seemed a little sad and I think Santa could sense that as well. Before even asking a question or saying hello, Santa engulfed him into a huge bear hug.

SANTA:

"Justin, dear boy, how are you tonight?" Santa whispered.

"I miss my Mom and Dad" Justin whispered back. "They're both deployed right now and I miss them very much. I know they can't make it home this year for Christmas, and that's okay. My grandparents take really good care of me. But, well..." he hesitated.

"Go ahead, ask your question." Santa encouraged Justin.

"Will you go visit them both for me and give them these?" Justin asked, and held out his hand. In them were two thimbles. Kisses, for those of us who remembered the story of Peter Pan. Justin explained, "They're thimbles, from our favorite bedtime story, and they represent a kiss. Can you make sure my parents get a kiss from me for Christmas?" he asked hopefully.

In response, Santa carefully took both the thimbles, and nodded "It would be my pleasure to deliver such a precious gift to your parents. They'll be home soon, so hang in there and keep being the wonderful grandson and son I know you are." Santa responded to Justin.

NOTES:

Our town is small, and we all know that Justin's parents are amazing examples of what it means to be selfless. We all have decorated each of our trees with a yellow ribbon, showing our love and respect for them while they're gone. It takes a village to raise our kids and we all keep an eye out for Justin during this trying time.

Last up is Kyle, he's skinny with a bowl haircut and knobby knees. He makes his way up to Santa and we're all a little curious to hear what the very last question of the evening is.

SANTA:

"Come on up Kyle!" Santa smiled. "Thank you for being so patient! Let's hear your question."

"Santa? What am I supposed to do when someone tells me that you're not real?" Kyle asks.

NOTES:

You could hear a pin drop at this very moment. I don't think anyone expected this question and I think a few older siblings and parents are feeling a little guilty at this very moment for having this conversation already with their kids and younger siblings. This question and its answer seem to spark such emotional responses in people, and I think we're all curious and a little timid to hear his answer.

SANTA:

"Well, now that is an exceptionally wonderful question, Kyle. I'm only one person, so there's a reason why you'll see Santa's at the mall or at Christmas parties. Santa is everywhere because Santa is the Spirit of Christmas and the Spirit of Giving. When you become old enough

yourself, you can become Santa by embodying the spirit of the season.

If someone tells you I'm not real, you can let them believe what they wish, and you believe what you wish. The Spirit of Christmas and the Season of Giving will never disappear so long as wonderful people such as yourself continue to believe in what you cannot see. For we cannot see love and yet, we know it is there."

NOTES:

With that, Kyle scurried off to his family, while Santa stood up to address us all.

SANTA:

"Thank you all for coming and allowing me the chance to connect with you all. It has been wonderful to see such amazing love all in one room!"

He straightened his suit a little, "You're welcome to tell this story if you wish, Mr. James, I know you've been taking your notes there in the back. Do me one favor please, should you publish this is a book, please take the money and donate it to a worthy cause."

SANTA:

I looked up, startled that Santa knew what I was up to the entire time and feeling a little like I had been caught. "Yes sir. My wife and I always donate to our local families in need and often buy gifts for kids that wouldn't get presents otherwise. We find local 'Angel Trees' and help out as many kids as we're able. Would you approve of me putting the proceeds to that?" I asked.

"That sounds exactly like something a Santa would do!" he replied to me. I blushed at such a compliment.

"Now, please help yourselves to more refreshments. I've packaged everything up so each of you have a box of goodies to take home. May you all become Santa's one day. Merry Christmas!" Santa boomed and clapped his hands in front of his face.

There was a flash of the white crackling light that his magic had become, and he and his chair were gone. He left only the gifts of food at the back and our hearts full of love. As we all slowly piled out of the library, we all knew in our own way that we'd never be the same.

FINAL NOTE:

It's been a year since we had that amazing visit, and I kept the story with our small town. Just so we could savor it a little longer. Now it's time to share it with the world so that we may all become Santa's in our own time.

And for those who would like to know, Justin's parents made it home safely around January 2nd, both with a thimble on a necklace around their neck. A kiss from their loving son, until they were able to return home.

As this notebook hits the shelves this holiday season, all the proceeds will go to keeping the Spirit of Christmas alive for those kids in need this holiday season and every holiday season afterwards.

A Merry Christmas to you,

Raymond "Ray" James

Did you enjoy this book?

You can help make a difference for the author by showing your support!

Reviews are the most powerful tool in an author's arsenal when it comes to getting attention for their books. Honest reviews help bring the attention of other readers and spread the word so more people can enjoy the stories authors have to tell.

If you enjoyed this book, please consider taking a minute or two to leave a review on any of your sites.

We appreciate your support!

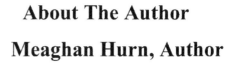

About The Author

Meaghan Hurn, Author

In my previous aspirations, I've been a Chef, Designer, Division1 Swimmer, Musician, Artist, Event Planner, MMA Amateur Fighter, Philosopher and Publisher and Author.

I love loose leaf teas, I collect teacups and coffee mugs, and strangely I love big soup spoons. I watch tons of documentaries, generally anything to do with oceanography and marine biology, military history and philosophy. I'm also a sucker for terrible dad jokes and puns.

Typically, I'm busy running my company, but when I'm not, you'll find me reading, playing an instrument, or listening to music. I'm also not a fan of small talk. I like to jump into the middle of a conversation and get the heart of a topic.

So, feel free to reach out and start a conversation!

www.meaghanhurn.com

About The Book Designer
Triumph Book Covers
Diana Toledo Calcado, Designer

My name is Diana T. Calcado and I'm a book cover designer and a book lover. What would I do if I had all the time in the world? You guessed it: Read ,many, many books!

Having an artistic family, growing up I was always encouraged to learn a variety of different types of art, from metal embossing to painting ceramic tiles. This gave me the encouragement I needed to start learning digital art for my own book covers and for other authors as well.

Whether this is your very first book or you're an experienced author with many published books under your belt, I will help you create a cover that you will love.

www._triumphbookcovers.com
www.facebook.com/triumphcovers

About The Publisher

Hurn Publications is the proud publisher of great writers and gifted

storytellers, beloved books and eminent works. We believe that literature can fuel the imagination and guide the soul. There is a book on our shelves for every reader, and we relish the opportunity to publish across every category and interest with the utmost care, attention to diverse inclusion and enthusiasm.

Find your next great read: www.hurnpublications.com

HP Newsletter Signup

Signing up for our newsletter gets you Book Reviews, Books On Tour, Cover Reveals, Giveaways and Book Sales delivered right to your inbox.

Stay up to date in the Indie Publishing world!

Link: https://www.subscribepage.com/hurnpublications

CPSIA information can be obtained
at www.ICGtesting.com
Printed in the USA
BVHW020957131220
595305BV00001B/4